The Kind of Love That Grows in Silence

A Poetic Love Story

Kota Naga Rohith

The Kind of Love That Grows in Silence
A Poetic Love Story

ISBN- 13: 978-93-343-9605-8

Cover design: Kota Naga Rohith
Book layout: Kota Naga Rohith

Published by Independently published

This is a work of fiction. Any resemblance to actual events, places, or persons, living or dead, is purely coincidental.

First Edition, 2025

For Sundari —
the silence where love found its voice.

Acknowledgments

With gratitude to the quiet moments, the long walks, the river conversations, and the people who reminded me that love does not always need to be loud to be true.

Thank you to my family and friends who encouraged me to write, and to Special Person, for being both muse and mirror.

About the Author

Kota Naga Rohith is a Salesforce Business Analyst and writer based in Essen, Germany. He holds a Master's degree in Big Data & Business Analytics and works in digital transformation projects while pursuing his creative passions in writing, photography, and storytelling.

"The Kind of Love That Grows in Silence" is his debut poetic love story — a novel that blends lived experiences with lyrical reflections on love, silence, and time.

When not writing, Rohith can be found with his camera capturing cityscapes, reading about design and entrepreneurship, or exploring cafés in search of the perfect coffee.

The Kind of Love That Grows in Silence

A Novel

Prologue: A Love That Didn't Arrive Loudly

Some love stories begin with sparks flying across crowded rooms, with dramatic declarations under starlit skies, with the kind of passion that burns bright and fast.

Ours began with silence.

A swipe on a screen. A profile that made me pause—not because of her beauty, though she was beautiful, but because of something in her eyes that seemed to say, *I have stories to tell, but only to the right person.*

A name: Elena.

A first message that didn't try to impress with witty one-liners or calculated charm. Just: *"I noticed you like that little café on Fifth Street. Their lavender latte is terrible, but the corner booth has the best light for reading. What do you think makes a perfect reading spot?"*

I stared at that message for twenty minutes before responding. Not because I didn't know what to say, but because I recognized something in it—a gentleness that the world had been rough with. A carefulness that spoke of someone who had learned that the best things are often the most fragile.

I didn't know then that this would become the story I'd write when I had no more words left in me—only feelings that refused to stay quiet any longer.

She wasn't a storm that would tear through my life, rearranging everything in her path.

She was a slow sky clearing after years of rain, and I was learning how to breathe again.

For the ones who felt everything but said nothing.

This one is for us.

Table of Contents

Chapter 1: The Kind of Love That Grows in Silence

The café on Fifth Street was everything Elena had promised—worn leather chairs that held the shape of a thousand readers, walls lined with books that looked loved rather than displayed, and yes, terrible lavender lattes that somehow tasted better when you weren't drinking them alone.

When I first saw her walk through the door, I didn't think, *This is it. This is the moment my life changes.*

I just noticed how she moved—unhurried, but purposeful. How she smiled at the barista with genuine warmth, not the performative politeness most of us wear like armor. How she looked around the room until her eyes found mine, and how that search ended with a smile that felt like recognition.

"You must be Kota," she said, sliding into the seat across from me. "I'm Elena. And before you ask—no, I didn't order the lavender latte. I have a policy against subjecting nice people to unnecessary suffering on first meetings."

I laughed—not the careful, measured laugh of someone trying to make a good impression, but the kind that surprised me with its honesty. "Does that policy extend to second meetings?"

"We'll have to see if you survive the first one."

Our conversation unfolded like a slow dance. She told me about her work as a graphic designer, how she'd moved to the city three years ago with dreams bigger than her savings account and how she'd learned to find beauty in uncertainty. I shared stories about my writing, the novel I'd been working on for two years, and how some days the blank page felt like an old friend and others like an accusation.

But it was the spaces between our words that drew me in. The comfortable pauses where she'd stir her coffee thoughtfully, or the way she'd look out the window and smile at something only she could see. Most people filled silence with noise, as if quiet were something to be conquered. Elena inhabited it like a natural space.

After two hours and multiple refills of decidedly better coffee than advertised, we walked to the river that wound through the heart of downtown. The Saturday afternoon buzzed around us—joggers in bright athletic wear, families with strollers, street musicians competing for attention—but we moved through it all like we were in our own quiet bubble.

"Do you ever feel," Elena said, stopping to lean against the stone railing overlooking the water, "like most conversations are just people waiting for their turn to talk? Like everyone's so focused on what they're going to say next that they forget to actually listen?"

I watched the way the afternoon light caught the auburn threads in her dark hair. "All the time. It's like everyone's performing instead of connecting."

"Exactly." She turned to face me fully, and I felt the weight of being truly seen. "I used to think I was bad at conversation because I didn't always have something clever to say. But maybe I was just looking for something different."

"What were you looking for?"

She was quiet for a long moment, her fingers tracing patterns on the stone. "Someone who could sit in the quiet spaces without needing to fill them. Someone who understood that sometimes the most important things can't be said—only felt."

We fell into one of those quiet spaces then, watching the water catch and scatter sunlight like scattered thoughts. It should have been awkward—two strangers standing in silence on their first meeting. Instead, it felt like the most natural thing in the world.

That's when I realized something that would change everything: I didn't want this afternoon to end. Not because of what we'd said, but because of what we hadn't needed to say.

Elena didn't enter my life like others had—with fanfare and expectations and the exhausting energy of trying to impress. She arrived like a pause in a song I didn't realize I'd been humming, a moment of stillness that made me understand why I'd been rushing.

And suddenly, I didn't want to skip forward anymore.

As we walked back toward the café where our cars were parked, she said, "I had a really lovely time today, Kota. Thank you."

"Me too," I said, and meant it in a way that surprised me with its depth.

"Would you..." she started, then paused, a slight blush coloring her cheeks. "Would you like to do this again sometime? Maybe somewhere with better coffee?"

"I'd love that," I said. "Though I have to warn you—I'm developing a strange fondness for terrible lavender lattes."

Her laugh was like sunlight breaking through clouds. "Well, then I guess we'll have to find new ways to suffer together."

As I drove home that evening, I found myself replaying not the things she'd said, but the way she'd said them. The thoughtfulness behind each word, the care she took with silence, the way she made space for both of us in every conversation.

I'd been on dates before. I'd felt attraction, interest, even infatuation. But this felt different—quieter and somehow more certain. Like the difference between a firework and a star: one burns bright and brief, the other provides steady light for navigation.

That night, I lay awake not because I was overthinking what had happened, but because I was savoring it. Rolling the memory of her laugh around in my mind like a smooth stone worn by water, something to hold onto in the dark.

I didn't know then that this was how it would always be with Elena—not the dramatic highs and lows of passion, but the deep, steady current of something real building slowly, carefully, in the spaces between what we said and what we meant.

Some love stories begin with lightning strikes.

Ours began with the patient work of learning each other's silence.

Poetic Echo

"I have spread my dreams under your feet;
Tread softly because you tread on my dreams."
— W.B. Yeats

Chapter 2: The Space Between Almost and Always

Three weeks later

We fell into a rhythm as natural as breathing.

Tuesday evenings became badminton at the community center—neither of us particularly skilled, but both competitive enough to keep it interesting. Elena had a way of celebrating my rare good shots that made me feel like I'd just won Wimbledon, and when she beat me (which was most of the time), her victory dances were elaborate enough to make the loss worthwhile.

"You're letting me win," she accused one evening, wiping sweat from her forehead with the back of her hand.

"I'm absolutely not," I protested, though we both knew my backhand had gotten mysteriously worse over the past week.

"Kota." She fixed me with a look that was part amusement, part exasperation. "I may not be a professional athlete, but I'm not stupid. That last shot? You practically handed it to me."

I tried to look innocent. "Maybe you're just getting better."

"Maybe you're just getting more transparent." She grabbed her water bottle and settled onto the bench beside me, close enough that I could smell her shampoo—something clean and citrusy that I'd started associating with contentment. "I don't need you to let me win, you know. I'm perfectly capable of beating you honestly."

"I know," I said. "I just... I like seeing you celebrate."

The admission hung in the air between us, more honest than I'd intended. Elena turned to study my face, and I felt heat rise in my cheeks.

"You like seeing me celebrate," she repeated slowly, like she was testing the words.

"Is that weird?"

"It's..." She paused, seeming to choose her words carefully. "It's sweet. And a little dangerous."

"Dangerous how?"

"Because it makes me want to celebrate more things with you."

Fridays became dinner nights—nothing fancy, just whatever restaurant caught our eye. We developed a system: she'd choose the place, I'd choose the wine (though Elena's definition of "wine" was generous enough to include the occasional craft beer or creative cocktail). These weren't dates, exactly, because neither of us had called them that. They were just... time spent together. Time we both seemed to crave without discussing why.

One Friday, we found ourselves at a tiny Vietnamese restaurant tucked between a dry cleaner and a used bookstore. The pho was excellent, but what I remember most is how Elena ate—thoughtfully, pausing between bites to tell me about her latest project or to ask about the chapter I was struggling with.

"What's the hardest part?" she asked. "About writing, I mean."

I considered the question while fishing noodles out of my bowl. "The space between what you want to say and what actually comes out on the page. It's like... you have this perfect story in your head, but the moment you try to capture it in words, something gets lost in translation."

"Like trying to describe a sunset to someone who's never seen one?"

"Exactly. You can say 'orange and pink and beautiful,' but that doesn't even come close to what it actually is."

Elena nodded slowly. "I think the design is similar. You have this vision of how something should feel, but then you're limited by fonts and colors and space. Sometimes the most important part of a design is what you leave out."

"The negative space."

"The negative space," she agreed. "Sometimes emptiness says more than content."

It was one of those conversations that seemed simple on the surface but left me thinking for days afterward. Not because of what we'd discussed, but because of how naturally we'd understood each other, how seamlessly her thoughts had connected with mine.

Saturday mornings became coffee walks—not at the café where we'd met, but at a farmer's market that was set up in the park near Elena's apartment. We'd get cortados from a local roaster and wander between stalls of fresh vegetables and handmade jewelry, talking about everything and nothing.

It was during one of these walks, as we paused to let a family with a stroller pass, that Elena said something that would echo in my mind for weeks.

"Do you ever feel like life is waiting to tell you something, but it keeps whispering instead of shouting?"

We'd stopped beside a vendor selling succulents—tiny plants in hand-painted pots that looked impossibly delicate and surprisingly resilient. I picked up a small jade plant, turning it over in my hands while I considered her question.

"I do," I said finally. "Maybe some things are meant to be heard only in silence."

Elena smiled—not the bright, celebratory smile from badminton victories, but something sadder and more knowing. "That's what I'm afraid of."

"Why afraid?"

"Because I've never been very good at listening to whispers. I'm always waiting for life to be more obvious about what it wants from me."

I set the plant down carefully and looked at her—really looked. There was something vulnerable in her expression, something that made me want to step closer and promise that some whispers were worth learning to hear.

Instead, I said, "Maybe life doesn't want to be obvious. Maybe the whispers are the point."

"What do you mean?"

"Maybe the things worth having are the ones that make you pay attention. The ones that require you to be still and listen carefully."

She was quiet for a long moment, her fingers trailing over the smooth leaves of a succulent. "That's a nice way to think about it."

We bought plants that day—here a small echeveria with pink-edged leaves, me the jade plant I'd been holding. As we walked back to our cars, Elena said, "I'm going to put this on my windowsill and see if I can keep it alive. Think of it as practice for paying attention to quiet things."

"I think you're better at that than you realize," I said.

"We'll see."

That night, I placed my jade plant on the kitchen counter where the morning light would hit it first. Such a small thing—a plant, a conversation, a smile that lingered in my memory longer than it should have. But small things, I was learning, could carry unexpected weight.

That was us—caught in the space between almost and always. We hadn't kissed. We hadn't confessed anything beyond friendship. We hadn't defined what we were doing or where it was leading.

But there was gravity between us, a pull that grew stronger with each shared silence, each comfortable laugh, each moment when our hands accidentally brushed and neither of us pulled away quickly.

In that in-between space, I felt everything: longing, joy, anticipation, fear. The fear that if I reached across that invisible distance and took her hand, I might break whatever delicate thing we were building. The joy that came from simply being in her presence. The longing for more—more time, more conversation, more of the quiet understanding that seemed to flow between us without effort.

So I stayed in the almost. In the ache of unspoken feelings and careful distances. In the quiet rhythm of a love story that was never loud but somehow felt more real than anything that had come before.

We were learning each other slowly, the way you learn a new language—not through textbooks and grammar rules, but through immersion and practice and the gradual recognition that some things can only be understood through experience.

And if sometimes I lay awake at night wondering what it would feel like to tell Elena how I really felt, to close the space between almost and always—well, that was just another whisper I was learning to hear.

Poetic Echo

"Love is anterior to life, Posterior to death,

Initial of Creation, and The exponent of breath."

— Emily Dickinson

Chapter 3: When a Hug Meant Everything

My birthday - October 15th

I wasn't planning to make a big deal of it. Birthdays had always felt complicated to me—too much pressure to feel celebratory, too many expectations about marking the passage of time in meaningful ways. But when Elena asked what I was doing to celebrate, something in her voice made me want to include her in whatever small recognition I could muster.

"Probably just dinner somewhere quiet," I'd told her over text. "Nothing fancy."

Her response came immediately: "Would you like some company? I make excellent dinner conversations and terrible birthday wishes."

"How terrible are we talking?"

"The kind that are so earnest they're embarrassing. Consider yourself warned."

We met at a small Italian restaurant I'd been meaning to try—the kind of place with checkered tablecloths and wine bottles converted to candle holders, where the menu was written on a chalkboard and everything smelled like garlic and possibility. Elena arrived first, which surprised me since I'd developed a habit of being early for our meetings, as if those extra few minutes of anticipation were part of the pleasure.

I saw her through the window before I entered, sitting at a corner table with her hands wrapped around a water glass, watching the door with an expression I couldn't quite read. When she spotted me, her face broke into a smile that made me understand why people wrote songs about such things.

"Happy birthday," she said as I approached the table. "You look exactly one year older."

"Thanks, I think."

"It's a good look on you. Very distinguished."

Dinner unfolded with the same easy rhythm our evenings had developed—conversation flowing between serious and silly, comfortable silences punctuated by laughter, the kind of time that passes without your awareness because you're exactly where you want to be.

But something felt different that night. Maybe it was the soft lighting, or the wine Elena had insisted on ordering ("It's your birthday, Kota, we're being fancy"), or the way she seemed to be studying my face when she thought I wasn't looking. There was an intensity to her attention that made me hyperaware of every word I spoke, every gesture I made.

"Can I ask you something?" she said as we split a piece of tiramisu that neither of us had room for but both agreed looked too good to pass up.

"Of course."

"What's the best birthday you ever had?"

I thought about it while savoring a forkful of mascarpone and coffee-soaked ladyfingers. "When I was eight, my grandmother took me to the natural history museum. Just the two of us. We spent the whole day looking at dinosaurs and meteorites, and she let me choose something from the gift shop."

"What did you choose?"

"A geode. This ugly gray rock that looked like nothing special until you cracked it open and found all these purple crystals inside." I smiled at the memory. "My grandmother said it was a good metaphor for people—that sometimes the most beautiful things are hidden where you least expect them."

Elena's expression softened. "She sounds wonderful."

"She was. She died when I was fifteen, but I still have that geode. It's on my bookshelf at home."

"What made that birthday special? Besides the geode?"

I considered the question. "I think it was feeling completely understood. Like my grandmother saw exactly who I was—this quiet kid who preferred rocks to toys and museums to playgrounds—and loved that person instead of trying to change him."

Elena nodded slowly. "That's a beautiful gift."

"What about you? Best birthday?"

"Last year," she said without hesitation.

"What happened last year?"

"Nothing. That was the point." She laughed, but there was something serious underneath it. "I'd just gotten out of this relationship that had been... complicated. Drama-heavy. My ex wanted to throw me this big party, invite all these people I barely knew, make it into this performance of how amazing and popular I was. And I realized I didn't want any of that."

"What did you want?"

"To be alone with my thoughts. To order Chinese food and watch old movies and not have to perform happiness for anyone." She paused. "It was the first birthday where I felt like I could just be myself without apologizing for it."

"And that was enough?"

"It was everything."

When the check came, I reached for it automatically, but Elena's hand covered mine. "Please. Let me get this. It's your birthday."

"You don't have to—"

"I want to. Consider it my gift to eight-year-old you and the grandmother who taught you to look for beautiful hidden things."

After dinner, we walked to my car in the parking lot behind the restaurant. The October air had the crisp edge of approaching winter, and Elena wrapped her cardigan tighter around herself as we walked.

"Thank you," I said when we reached my car. "For dinner, for the company, for making this feel special without making it feel like work."

"Thank you for letting me be part of it."

We stood there in the parking lot, neither of us quite ready to end the evening. The space between us felt charged with something I couldn't name—expectation, maybe, or possibility. Like we were standing at the edge of something important, waiting to see who would step forward first.

And then Elena moved closer.

Not dramatically, not with the purposeful stride of someone making a grand gesture. Just a small step that closed the distance between us from arm's length to something much more intimate.

"Happy birthday, Kota," she said softly.

And then she hugged me.

It wasn't a quick, friendly embrace. It wasn't the polite hug of acquaintances or the casual affection of established friends. It was slow, deliberate, and quietly intense. Her arms wound around my shoulders, pulling me close enough that I could feel her heartbeat against my chest. Her face nestled into the space between my neck and shoulder, and her breath was warm against my skin.

I wrapped my arms around her waist, holding her close, and felt something shift between us—something that had been building for weeks finally finding expression in the simple act of two bodies recognizing their need for closeness.

She didn't pull away quickly. Neither did I.

We stood there in that parking lot, holding each other like we were afraid the other might disappear if we loosened our grip. Time seemed suspended, the world reduced to the circle of warmth we created together.

I could smell her perfume—something subtle and clean that I'd never noticed before but knew I'd remember forever. I could feel the slight tremble in her breathing, the way her fingers pressed against my back like she was trying to memorize the shape of me.

When we finally separated, it was reluctantly, with the kind of slow reluctance that suggested we both wished we didn't have to.

"Thank you," I said, though the words felt inadequate for what had just passed between us.

"Thank you," she echoed, her voice softer than usual.

We looked at each other for a moment—really looked, without the casual pretense of friendship to hide behind. Her eyes were bright in the parking lot lights, and I thought I saw something there that matched the feeling growing in my chest.

"I should go," she said, though she made no move toward her car.

"Yeah," I agreed, making no move toward mine.

Finally, with what seemed like considerable effort, Elena stepped back. "Drive safe, birthday boy."

"You too."

I waited until she was safely in her car before getting into mine, but even after she'd driven away, I sat in that parking lot for another ten minutes, replaying every second of that embrace.

That hug became my safe place—a memory I would return to on difficult days, in lonely moments, whenever I needed proof that connection was possible. It wasn't a confession of love, wasn't a promise of anything more than what we already had.

But it was something. Something real and honest and worth holding onto.

And for the first time since I'd met Elena, I allowed myself to believe that maybe—just maybe—she felt it too.

Poetic Echo

"The minute I heard my first love story, I started looking for you...
Not knowing how blind that was. Lovers don't finally meet
somewhere. They're in each other all along."

— Rumi

Chapter 4: She Felt Like Home, Then Left the Door Ajar

November

The shift was so gradual I almost convinced myself I was imagining it.

It started with response times. Elena, who used to text back within minutes, began taking hours to reply. Her messages were still warm, still thoughtful, but they felt different somehow—like she was editing herself, choosing words more carefully.

"How was your day?" became "Busy day, hope yours was good."

"That made me think of you" became "Saw this and remembered our conversation."

Small changes. Probably meaningless. I told myself I was overthinking, that people got busy, that not every shift in communication meant something significant.

But then our Tuesday badminton games started getting canceled.

"Client emergency, rain check?"

"Feeling under the weather, better skip this week."

"A family thing came up, so sorry!"

Each excuse was perfectly reasonable. Each cancellation came with genuine apologies and suggestions to reschedule that never quite materialized into actual plans.

By mid-November, we'd gone two weeks without seeing each other in person.

I found myself checking my phone more often, crafting and deleting messages I never sent, wondering if I'd done something wrong or if Elena was simply losing interest in whatever we'd been building together.

The hardest part was remembering how she used to make me feel. Like coming home after a long journey. Like I could breathe deeper in her presence. She'd told me I had the same effect on her—that being with me felt calm, safe, real in a way that was rare for her.

"You make me feel like I don't have to perform," she'd said one evening after badminton, as we sat in my car in the community center parking lot, neither of us ready to end the night. "Like I can just be myself, even the quiet, weird parts."

"Your quiet, weird parts are my favorite parts," I'd replied, meaning it completely.

She'd looked at me then with something that felt like tenderness, like gratitude, like possibility. "That's dangerous, you know."

"Why is it dangerous?"

"Because it makes me want to show you more of them."

Now, three weeks later, I wondered if she'd changed her mind about that. If the quiet, weird parts of herself had started to feel too vulnerable, too exposed. If whatever connection we'd found had begun to feel like too much risk for not enough certainty.

The worst part wasn't the silence—it was the half-communication. Elena never disappeared completely. She still responded to my messages, still liked my social media posts, and still maintained the thread of connection between us. But she did it all from behind an invisible wall that I couldn't name or navigate.

She never said goodbye. She never closed the door. She just left it ajar—wide enough for me to hope we could find our way back to each other, but not wide enough for me to actually enter the space we'd been building.

And me? I stayed on the doorstep.

Not knocking insistently. Not demanding explanations or clarity. Just... waiting.

One evening in late November, after five days without any communication, I finally called her. The phone rang four times before going to voicemail, and I almost hung up without leaving a message. But something about her recorded voice—warm and familiar and somehow distant—made me want to try.

"Hey, it's me," I said after the beep. "I was just thinking about that terrible lavender latte from our first meeting, and I wondered if you ever went back to that café. Anyway, I... I hope you're doing well. Call me back when you can."

She texted an hour later: "Sorry, missed your call. Café closed down, actually. Kind of sad. Hope you're well too."

Eleven words. Perfectly polite, completely distant. No mention of seeing each other, no suggestion that she missed our conversations or Tuesday night games or the easy rhythm we'd developed.

I stared at that message for twenty minutes, typing and deleting responses. "I miss you." Delete. "Did I do something wrong?" Delete. "Can we talk about what's happening?" Delete.

Finally, I sent back: "That is sad. Take care of yourself."

Three weeks later, I drove past the café where we'd met. Elena was right—it was closed, with brown paper covering the windows and a "For Lease" sign in the door. Seeing it empty felt like a metaphor I didn't want to examine too closely.

But I couldn't stop myself from parking across the street and sitting there for a few minutes, remembering how nervous I'd been that first day, how Elena's smile had put me at ease, how the terrible coffee had somehow tasted perfect because she was there to share it.

That's the thing about someone who feels like home—you don't leave, even when they stop answering the door. You don't pack up your feelings and move on to the next person who might want them. You stay, hoping that whatever made them withdraw might eventually resolve itself, that the door might open again.

Because love, the real kind, doesn't walk away when things get complicated. It waits.

Even if it means standing in the cold, watching windows that used to be warm with light, wondering if the person inside can see you there and if they want you to stay or go.

Even if waiting starts to feel like its own kind of heartbreak.

I stayed because I loved her. Not the idea of her, not the potential of what we might become, but her—Elena with her thoughtful silences and victory dances and the way she could make me feel understood with a single glance.

And love, I was learning, doesn't give up on people just because they give up on themselves.

Even if it has to wait outside, in the space between almost and never, hoping for another chance to come home.

Poetic Echo

"The best way out is always through."

— Robert Frost

Chapter 5: A Kiss That Lingered in Thought, Not Lips

December

The almost-kiss happened on a Tuesday.

After three weeks of distance and careful text messages, Elena had finally agreed to meet for coffee. Not at our usual place (which had closed), and not with the easy familiarity we'd once shared, but it was something. A crack in the door she'd been keeping ajar.

We met at a chain coffee shop near her work—the kind of place that was efficient and anonymous, where everything was designed for quick transactions rather than lingering conversations. Not exactly romantic, but I was so grateful to see her face that I wouldn't have cared if we were meeting in a parking garage.

She looked tired, I noticed. Beautiful, but tired. Like she hadn't been sleeping well or had been carrying weight she didn't know how to set down.

"Thank you for meeting me," I said as we found seats at a small table by the window.

"Of course." She wrapped her hands around her coffee cup like she was trying to warm herself from the inside out. "I'm sorry I've been so... distant lately."

"You don't have to apologize. I just wanted to make sure you were okay."

She smiled, but it didn't quite reach her eyes. "I'm fine. Just busy with work and figuring some things out."

"Anything I can help with?"

"No, it's... it's nothing specific. Just life stuff, you know?"

I wanted to push, to ask what kind of life stuff made someone withdraw from people who cared about them. But Elena's body language was careful, guarded, and I didn't want to risk making her retreat further by pressing too hard.

So we talked about safe things. Her latest design project. The novel I was still struggling to finish. The early December weather couldn't decide if it wanted to be autumn or winter. Surface-level conversation that felt nothing like the deep, meandering talks we used to share.

But underneath the careful politeness, I could feel something else. A tension, like the air before a thunderstorm. Elena kept glancing at me when she thought I wasn't looking, and whenever our eyes met directly, she'd look away quickly, a slight flush coloring her cheeks.

After an hour of this careful dance, I suggested we take a walk. The coffee shop was crowded and noisy, and I thought maybe the movement and fresh air might help us find our way back to something more genuine.

We ended up in the small park across from her office building—just a couple of benches and a fountain that had been turned off for the season. The December air was sharp and clean, and Elena pulled her coat tighter around herself as we walked the perimeter path.

"I've missed this," she said suddenly, breaking a comfortable silence.

"Walking?"

"No, just... being with you. Without having to think so hard about every word I say."

The admission hung between us, more honest than anything she'd shared in weeks.

"I've missed you too," I said. "More than I probably should admit."

She stopped walking then, turning to face me with an expression I couldn't quite read. We were standing beneath a streetlight that cast everything in golden winter light, and for a moment, the carefully maintained distance between us seemed to collapse.

"Kota," she said, and my name sounded different in her voice. Softer. More vulnerable.

"Yeah?"

"I need to tell you something."

My heart started beating faster. "Okay."

But instead of speaking, she just looked at me. Really looked like she was trying to memorize my face or gather courage for whatever she needed to say.

The space between us felt charged, electric in a way that made me hyperaware of every detail: the way her breath made small clouds in the cold air, the slight tremor in her hands, the way she kept glancing at my mouth and then back to my eyes.

I took a step closer. She didn't step back.

"Elena," I said softly.

"I know," she whispered, though I hadn't actually said anything that needed knowing.

But somehow, she did know. She knew that standing this close to her was making it hard for me to remember why we'd been maintaining careful distances. She knew that the way she was looking at me was making me want to close the space between us completely.

She knew, because she was feeling the same thing.

I lifted my hand slowly, giving her plenty of time to pull away, and traced my fingers along her cheek. Her skin was cold from the winter air but warmed under my touch.

"Is this okay?" I asked.

She leaned into my touch instead of answering with words, and I felt something in my chest crack open.

We stood there like that for a moment—my hand on her face, her eyes closed, both of us breathing carefully like we were afraid sudden movements might break whatever spell we were under.

When she opened her eyes again, they were bright with something that looked like tears and desire and fear all mixed together.

"I should go," she said, but she made no move to step away from my touch.

"Should you?"

"I don't know. I don't know anything anymore."

The honesty in her voice nearly undid me. Here was the Elena I'd been missing—unguarded, uncertain, real.

I could have kissed her then. Every signal was there: the way she was looking at me, the way she hadn't pulled away from my touch, the way the space between us seemed to hum with possibility. If I had leaned down just a few inches, if I had closed that final distance between us...

But something held me back. Maybe it was the fear in her eyes alongside the desire. Maybe it was the knowledge that she'd been pulling away for weeks and I didn't want to push her into something she wasn't ready for. Maybe it was the understanding that some moments are too important to rush, too fragile to force.

Instead, I stroked my thumb across her cheekbone once, gently, and then let my hand drop to my side.

"When you're ready," I said quietly, "I'll be here."

The relief and disappointment that crossed her face in rapid succession told me I'd made the right choice, even if it wasn't the easy one.

"Thank you," she whispered.

We walked back to our cars in comfortable silence, but something fundamental had shifted between us. The almost-kiss had said things we weren't ready to speak aloud yet, had acknowledged feelings we were still learning how to hold.

I drove home that night carrying the memory of her skin under my fingertips, the weight of her trust in letting me that close, the knowledge that she wanted me to kiss her almost as much as I'd wanted to.

Almost.

That kiss—the one that existed only in pauses and glances and the space between intention and action—lived in my thoughts for weeks afterward. Not as a regret, but as a promise. A love letter written in the language of restraint and patience and caring more about someone's readiness than your own desire.

Some kisses happen in moments of passion, stealing breath and reason in equal measure.

Others happen in the space between heartbeats, in the choice not to take what isn't freely given, in the understanding that the most powerful moments are sometimes the ones that remain suspended in possibility.

And in a way, that almost-kiss—the one that lived only in intention and restraint—was more intimate than any kiss that had come before it. Because it held everything: desire and respect, longing and patience, love and the wisdom to let that love unfold in its own time.

Poetic Echo

"I want to do with you what spring does with the cherry trees."

— Pablo Neruda

Chapter 6: Love Without Labels

Christmas week

The text came on December 23rd, at 11:47 PM.

"Are you awake?"

I was, actually—lying in bed reading, or trying to read, mostly just thinking about Elena and whether she was spending the holidays with family or friends or alone. We'd exchanged a few messages since our almost-kiss in the park, careful check-ins that felt like two people learning how to navigate new territory without a map.

"I am now. Is everything okay?" I typed back.

"Can I call you?"

My heart did something complicated. "Of course."

The phone rang thirty seconds later.

"Hi," Elena's voice was soft, tentative.

"Hi. What's going on?"

"I couldn't sleep. I keep thinking about things."

"What kind of things?"

There was a long pause, and I could hear her breathing on the other end of the line. When she spoke again, her voice was even quieter.

"Us things. What we are, what we're not, what we might be."

I sat up in bed, suddenly more awake than I'd been in hours. "Want to talk about it?"

"I don't know how to talk about it. That's the problem."

"Try anyway. I'm good at figuring out what people mean even when they're not sure how to say it."

Another pause. Then: "What are we doing, Kota?"

"What do you mean?"

"I mean, we're not dating. We're not just friends. We're something else, something in between, and I don't know what to call it or how to explain it to myself, let alone to other people."

I thought about that—about the months of careful connection we'd built, the way we'd learned each other's rhythms and moods and silences. About badminton games and dinner conversations and text messages that felt more intimate than most physical contact I'd experienced.

"Does it need a name?" I asked.

"Doesn't everything?"

"I don't think so. I think some things are bigger than the words we use to contain them."

"But how do you know what something is if you can't name it?"

"How do you know what the color blue is? You can't really describe it to someone who's never seen it. You just... know it when you see it."

Elena was quiet for so long I started to wonder if she'd hung up.

"Are you still there?" I asked.

"I'm here. I'm just thinking about blue."

"What about it?"

"It's funny—you say you can't describe blue to someone who's never seen it, but we try anyway. We say it's like the sky or the ocean or sadness. We use metaphors and comparisons because even though they're inadequate, they're better than nothing."

"So what metaphors would you use for us?"

"I don't know. That's what's driving me crazy." Her laugh was self-deprecating. "I'm usually good with words, with defining things. But with you... it's like trying to hold water in my hands."

"Maybe that's okay."

"Is it?"

"Elena," I said, and something in my tone must have conveyed more seriousness because she went completely quiet. "What we have—whatever we want to call it or not call it—it's real. It matters. It's changed how I see the world and how I move through it. Isn't that enough?"

"It should be," she said. "But I'm scared."

"Of what?"

"Of not knowing where we're going. Of caring about someone without being able to define the relationship. Of..." She trailed off.

"Of what, Elena?"

"Of falling in love with someone when I don't even know if that's what we're doing."

The admission hung between us like a held breath. I felt something in my chest expand and contract simultaneously—joy at her honesty, fear at her fear, hope at the possibility she'd just named.

"Would that be so terrible?" I asked gently. "Falling in love?"

"It would be terrifying."

"Because of the uncertainty?"

"Because of you."

I didn't know what to say, so I waited.

"You're..." she started, then stopped. Started again. "You're not like anyone I've dated before. You're patient and kind and you pay attention to things most people miss. You make me feel seen in a way that's both wonderful and terrifying because once someone sees you that clearly, you can't go back to being invisible."

"I don't want you to be invisible."

"I know. That's what scares me."

We stayed on the phone for another hour, talking in circles around the thing we were both feeling but neither quite ready to name definitively. Elena told me about her family Christmas plans, about the novel she'd been reading, about the way winter made her want to hibernate until spring.

I told her about the short story I'd finished that week, about missing our Tuesday badminton games, about how the jade plant I'd bought at the farmer's market was somehow still alive despite my historically terrible relationship with keeping things green.

"I think about you," she said as we were winding down the call. "More than I should probably admit."

"How much is more than you should admit?"

"Daily. Sometimes hourly." She laughed, embarrassed. "God, that sounds pathetic."

"It sounds honest. And for what it's worth, I think about you too. Daily. Sometimes hourly. Sometimes every few minutes."

"Really?"

"Really."

"That's..." She paused. "That's not nothing, is it?"

"No," I said. "It's definitely not nothing."

After we hung up, I lay awake for another two hours, replaying the conversation and thinking about the space between friendship and love, between certainty and possibility, between what we were and what we might become.

Elena was right—what we had didn't fit neatly into conventional categories. We weren't dating in any traditional sense, but we also weren't "just friends." We were something else, something that existed in the spaces between established definitions.

But maybe that was okay. Maybe the most important things in life—love, connection, understanding—were too complex and individual to be captured by the limited vocabulary we used to organize our experiences.

Maybe what we had was exactly what it needed to be: undefined but real, unlabeled but meaningful, uncertain but worth pursuing.

Maybe love without labels was still love.

And maybe, sometimes, that was the most honest kind of all.

Poetic Echo

"I carry your heart with me (i carry it in my heart)"
— e.e. cummings

Chapter 7: When I Said 'I Love You' and Meant It Fully, Quietly

---

January 8th

It happened on a Tuesday afternoon in Elena's apartment.

We'd started seeing each other again—carefully, tentatively, but consistently. After our Christmas Eve phone call, something had shifted. Not dramatically, not with grand declarations or sudden clarity, but subtly, like the way seasons change. The careful distance Elena had been maintaining began to soften, and I found myself back in her life in small but meaningful ways.

Coffee dates became coffee dates at her place. Text conversations extended into phone calls that lasted until one of us noticed how late it had gotten. She started sending me pictures again—a sunrise from her bedroom window, a particularly ridiculous latte art at the coffee shop near her work, her houseplant (which, unlike mine, was thriving under her care).

On this particular Tuesday, she'd invited me over to help her rearrange her living room furniture. It was the kind of domestic intimacy we'd been building toward for months—not romantic in any obvious way, but comfortable and real and somehow more meaningful than dinner dates or planned activities.

"I think the couch should go there," Elena said, pointing to a spot near the window. "But I can't move it by myself, and I've been staring at this room for two weeks trying to figure out how to make it feel more like home."

"How long have you lived here again?"

"Three years." She laughed at herself. "I know, I know. You'd think I'd have figured out furniture placement by now."

"Maybe you just needed a second opinion."

"Maybe I needed an excuse to have you over without it being weird."

The admission surprised both of us, I think. Elena blushed immediately after saying it, and I felt that familiar warmth in my chest that came from her moments of unguarded honesty.

We spent the afternoon moving furniture and debating the optimal placement of everything from her bookshelf to her coffee table. Elena had strong opinions about spatial flow and natural light, while I mostly just lifted heavy things and offered encouragement. But there was something perfect about the mundane domesticity of it all—the way she measured spaces with her hands, the concentrated expression she got when trying to visualize how a room should feel, the way she asked for my input like my opinion genuinely mattered to her.

Around four o'clock, we collapsed onto her newly positioned couch, admiring our handiwork.

"Better?" I asked.

"So much better. I don't know why I waited so long to do this."

"Sometimes it takes another person to help you see what you need."

She turned to look at me, and something in her expression made the casual comment feel more significant than I'd intended. "Is that what you do? Help me see what I need?"

"I don't know. Do I?"

"Yeah," she said softly. "You do."

We were sitting close enough that I could see the flecks of gold in her brown eyes, and could count the freckles scattered across her nose. The afternoon light from her newly positioned window fell across her face in a way that made her look like a painting, something precious that belonged in a museum rather than a Tuesday afternoon furniture rearrangement session.

"Elena," I said.

"Yeah?"

And that's when it happened. Not in a moment of high drama or carefully planned romance, but in the middle of a simple afternoon, surrounded by furniture we'd spent hours arranging and rearranging.

"I love you."

The words came out quietly, without fanfare or expectation. Not because I was trying to be brave or romantic or make some grand gesture, but because keeping them inside had started to feel like holding my breath underwater. They needed to be spoken, needed to exist in the space between us rather than just in the private chambers of my heart.

Elena's eyes went wide, but not with fear. With something that looked like recognition, like she'd been waiting to hear those words even if she hadn't been ready to say them herself.

She didn't run. She didn't pull away or make excuses about needing to be somewhere else. She just... stayed. Looked at me with those gold-flecked eyes and stayed present in the moment I'd just created.

"Kota," she said, and my name sounded different in her voice. Gentler. More careful.

"I'm not saying it because I need you to say it back," I told her quickly. "I'm saying it because it's true, and I wanted you to know. You should know that you're loved. Fully and quietly and without conditions."

Her eyes filled with tears, but she was smiling. "You can't just say things like that."

"Why not?"

"Because it makes me want to believe in things I've been too scared to hope for."

"Maybe that's okay. Maybe being scared doesn't mean something's wrong—maybe it means it matters."

She reached for my hand then, threading her fingers through mine with the kind of careful intimacy that felt more significant than any dramatic gesture.

"I'm not ready to say it back," she said. "Not because I don't feel it, but because I need to be sure. Because when I say those words to you, I want to mean them the way you mean them—fully and quietly and without conditions."

"I can wait."

"You shouldn't have to wait."

"I'm not waiting for you to love me, Elena. I already love you. The waiting is just... existing alongside that love until you're ready to trust it."

She squeezed my hand, and we sat there in her rearranged living room, holding hands and holding space for feelings that were bigger than either of us knew how to handle alone.

"This is terrifying," she said.

"I know."

"But also..."

"Also?"

"Also the most honest thing anyone's ever said to me."

We stayed like that until the afternoon light faded into evening, talking about love and fear and the way feelings could be both wonderful and overwhelming. Elena made us grilled cheese sandwiches for dinner, and I helped her hang a piece of art she'd been meaning to put up for months.

It was the most ordinary extraordinary day I'd ever experienced.

When it came time for me to leave, Elena walked me to the door with a kind of reluctance that made me hope she was beginning to trust what we were building together.

"Thank you," she said as I put on my jacket.

"For what?"

"For saying it. For not making it about you needing something from me. For letting it just be what it is."

"What is it?"

"True," she said simply. "It's true, and it's beautiful, and I'm going to try to be brave enough to trust it."

I kissed her forehead—gently, briefly, the kind of kiss that says "I care about you" rather than "I want something from you"—and headed home.

That night, I lay awake not because I was anxious about Elena's response, but because I felt lighter than I had in months. I'd spoken my truth without agenda or expectation. I'd offered my love as a gift rather than a transaction.

And Elena had received it with the care and consideration it deserved.

Sometimes the most powerful words aren't the ones that get you what you want—they're the ones that let you become who you really are.

I loved Elena Martinez, fully and quietly and without conditions.

And now she knows.

Poetic Echo

"You were the poem I never knew how to write, and this life is the story I have always wanted to tell."

— Lang Leav

Chapter 8: The Days She Felt Distant

Late January

Love, I learned, is not a straight line.

After the afternoon when I told Elena I loved her, I expected... something. Not necessarily for her to say it back immediately, but maybe for the space between us to feel different, warmer, more certain. Instead, what followed were some of the most confusing weeks of our relationship.

Elena didn't withdraw completely, but she became careful again. Not in the cold, distant way she'd been in November, but with a different kind of caution—like someone who had just realized they were standing at the edge of a cliff and needed to decide whether to step forward or back away.

Our conversations became more measured. Where once we'd talked for hours about everything and nothing, now our phone calls felt structured, polite. She still responded to my texts, but her replies were shorter, more considered.

"How was your day?" I'd ask.

"Good, busy with work. Yours?"

"Fine. I worked on the novel for a few hours."

"That's great. Hope it went well."

Perfectly pleasant. Perfectly distant.

I started second-guessing everything. Had I pushed too hard by telling her I loved her? Had I made her feel pressured despite my assurances that I didn't need her to reciprocate? Was she pulling away because she didn't feel the same way, or because she did and that scared her?

The not knowing was its own kind of torture.

One evening in late January, after three days of particularly stilted text exchanges, I called her.

"Hi," she answered on the third ring, and even that single syllable sounded careful.

"Hi. How are you doing? Really doing, not just polite conversation doing."

There was a pause. "I'm okay. Why?"

"Because you feel far away lately. Not geographically—emotionally. And I'm wondering if I did something or said something that made you uncomfortable."

"You didn't do anything wrong."

"But something's different."

Another pause, longer this time. "Yes," she said finally. "Something is different."

"Can you tell me what?"

"I don't know how to explain it without sounding ridiculous."

"Try me. I'm good with ridiculous things."

I heard her take a deep breath. "When you told me you loved me, it was beautiful. Perfect, actually. You said all the right things, you didn't pressure me, you just... offered it freely. And I felt so grateful, so seen."

"But?"

"But then I started thinking about what it means. About what loving someone means and what being loved means and whether I'm capable of either one in the way you deserve."

My heart did something complicated. "Elena—"

"Let me finish, please. I've been thinking about all the ways I could hurt you, all the ways I could disappoint you, all the reasons you might realize you made a mistake. And I know that's not fair to either of us, but I can't seem to stop."

"What are you afraid of?"

"Everything," she said, and her voice cracked slightly. "I'm afraid of not being enough. I'm afraid of being too much. I'm afraid of loving you back and then losing you. I'm afraid of not loving you back and losing you anyway."

I sat with that for a moment, feeling the weight of her fear and wishing I could carry some of it for her.

"Can I tell you something?" I said finally.

"Okay."

"I'm scared too. Terrified, actually. Loving someone the way I love you is like handing them every weapon they could ever need to destroy you and trusting them not to use them. But you know what scares me more than that?"

"What?"

"Not loving you. Not taking this risk. Living my whole life wondering what might have been if I'd been brave enough to stay present with this feeling instead of protecting myself from it."

Elena was quiet for a long time. When she spoke again, her voice was smaller. "What if I'm not brave enough?"

"Then we figure it out together. Bravery isn't the absence of fear, Elena. It's being afraid and showing up anyway. And you've been showing up—maybe not perfectly, maybe not without reservation, but you've been showing up."

"It doesn't feel like enough."

"It's everything. Your presence, even when you're scared, is everything."

We talked for another hour, and gradually I felt some of the careful distance between us begin to dissolve. Elena told me about the voice in her head that catalogued all the ways relationships could go wrong, about her parents' messy divorce that had taught her love was something that ended badly more often than not, about her ex who had made her feel like she was never quite right—too quiet, too serious, too much work.

I told her about my own fears—about how much I wanted this to work and how that wanting sometimes felt like pressure, about the way love had always felt theoretical to me until I met her, about how I sometimes lay awake at night wondering if I was asking too much of someone who was still learning to trust.

By the end of the conversation, we hadn't solved anything, exactly, but we'd named the things that were making us both feel distant. And somehow, naming them made them feel more manageable.

"I don't want to feel this scared all the time," Elena said as we were winding down the call.

"You don't have to. Not all the time. Just when it matters. And I'll be here for those times."

"Even when I'm being ridiculous and overthinking everything?"

"Especially then."

The next few weeks were better. Not perfect—Elena still had days when the fear crept in and made her careful, still moments when I could feel her evaluating and re-evaluating every interaction between us. But she started letting me see those moments instead of hiding behind polite distance.

"I'm having one of those days," she'd text, and I'd know that meant she was swimming in anxiety about us, about herself, about the future.

"Want to talk about it or just want me to send you pictures of dogs doing ridiculous things?" I'd respond.

Usually she wanted both.

Love, I was learning, wasn't just about the beautiful moments of connection and understanding. It was also about showing up for someone's worst fears, their least rational thoughts, their 3 AM anxieties about whether they were worthy of being loved.

It was about staying present even when the other person couldn't quite believe you would.

And gradually, Elena's distant days became fewer and farther between. Not because her fears disappeared, but because she started trusting that I meant what I'd said that day in her living room—that I loved her fully and quietly and without conditions.

Even on the days when she couldn't love herself.

Poetic Echo

"A thing of beauty is a joy forever: Its loveliness increases; it will never Pass into nothingness."

— John Keats

Chapter 9: I Waited Without Asking Her to Stay

February

The thing about loving someone who's afraid of being loved is that patience becomes its own language.

Not the passive kind of waiting that's really just hope disguised as inaction, but active patience—the kind that shows up consistently without demanding proof that it's worth it. The kind that says, "I'm here," without adding, "but not forever unless you give me a reason to stay."

Elena was working through something I couldn't fix for her. I could see it in the way she sometimes looked at me—like she was trying to memorize my face while simultaneously calculating the distance to the nearest exit. Like she was fighting a war between wanting to trust me and the part of her that had learned to expect disappointment.

Some days she won that war. She'd text me first thing in the morning, or suggest we try a new restaurant, or send me a picture of something that made her think of me. Those days felt like sunlight breaking through clouds, like proof that whatever we were building was worth the careful construction.

Other days, the fear won. She'd go quiet for hours or days, responding to my messages with polite but distant replies that felt like someone pulling up a drawbridge. She'd cancel plans with reasonable excuses that were probably true but felt like practice for bigger cancellations.

And I waited.

Not because I was a saint or because I enjoyed uncertainty, but because I understood something about Elena that maybe she didn't fully see yet: her distance wasn't cruelty. It was protection. Self-preservation born from experiences I could only guess at.

So I developed a rhythm. I kept showing up without making it about me. When she went quiet, I gave her space while making it clear the space was temporary—a bridge she could cross back over whenever she was ready, not a permanent separation.

"No pressure," became my most frequently used phrase. "Just wanted you to know I'm thinking about you, no pressure to respond right away."

"Let me know if you want company, no pressure either way."

"Hope you're having a good day, no pressure to make it about me."

I kept living my life. I worked on my novel, made plans with friends, went to movies by myself when Elena wasn't available. Not as a strategy or to prove I didn't need her, but because loving someone doesn't mean dissolving yourself into that love.

But I also kept making space for her in that life. I turned down plans I would have enjoyed if they conflicted with times she was available. I learned her rhythms and honored them—she was always more open to connection in the mornings, more likely to retreat into herself in the evenings. She responded better to gentle check-ins than direct questions about her feelings.

One evening in mid-February, after she'd been particularly distant for three days, Elena called me out of nowhere.

"Hi," she said when I answered, and I could hear something fragile in her voice.

"Hi. Is everything okay?"

"I've been thinking."

"About what?"

"About how patient you are with me. About how I keep pulling away and you keep... not leaving."

I sat down on my couch, sensing this was a conversation that needed my full attention. "Should I be leaving?"

"Most people would have by now. Most people would have gotten tired of my... issues."

"I'm not most people."

"No, you're not." She was quiet for a moment. "Why? Why do you keep showing up when I keep making it difficult?"

The question felt important, like she was really asking whether my patience was sustainable or just elaborate manipulation disguised as kindness.

"Because I love you," I said. "Not the version of you that's easy to love, not the hypothetical you that doesn't struggle with trust and intimacy. I love you, Elena. The you that gets scared and pulls away. The you that fights internal battles I can't see or understand. The you that's doing the best she can with the tools she has."

I heard her breathing on the other end of the line, and I thought she might be crying.

"But also," I continued, "because I think you're worth waiting for. Not because you need to be fixed or because I'm trying to save you, but because what we have—even with all the uncertainty and careful distances—is already meaningful. It's already adding something to my life that wasn't there before."

"What if I never get better at this? What if I'm always going to be someone who struggles with letting people close?"

"Then we figure out how to build something beautiful within those constraints. Love isn't about becoming perfect for someone, Elena. It's about finding someone who can work with your imperfections while you work on them yourself."

"You make it sound simple."

"It's not simple. It's actually incredibly complicated and sometimes frustrating and occasionally heartbreaking. But it's also worth it. You're worth it."

Elena cried then—quietly, but I could hear it. And I sat on my couch holding the phone, wishing I could hold her instead but knowing that sometimes the most loving thing you can do is give someone space to feel their feelings without trying to fix them.

"I'm sorry," she said when the crying subsided.

"For what?"

"For being so difficult to love."

"Elena." I said her name firmly enough that she went quiet. "You are not difficult to love. You're careful about who gets to love you, which is different. You're protective of your heart, which makes sense. You're human, which means you're complicated and sometimes inconsistent and occasionally irrational. But difficult to love? No. You're one of the easiest people I've ever loved."

"Really?"

"Really. Loving you feels as natural as breathing. It's trusting that you want to be loved that's been the challenge."

We talked for two more hours that night, and something shifted between us. Not dramatically—Elena didn't suddenly become someone who never doubted our connection. But she stopped apologizing for being careful. She started trusting that my patience was genuine rather than strategic.

And I learned that waiting for someone doesn't mean putting your life on hold. It means making space in your life for their timeline while continuing to live fully on your own.

It means understanding that love isn't always ready when we are, but that doesn't make it less real.

It means choosing to see someone's caution as self-awareness rather than rejection.

Most importantly, it means believing that the best things in life are worth the time they take to develop properly—like wine, like friendships, like the kind of love that grows slowly and roots deeply and lasts.

Elena was worth waiting for.

But more than that, what we were building together was worth taking the time to build right.

Poetic Echo

"In secret we met— In silence I grieve."

— Lord Byron

Chapter 10: Almosts That Shaped My Heart

Early March

Some people break your heart with dramatic endings—fights that crescendo into slammed doors, betrayals that shatter everything you thought you knew, love that burns hot and dies sudden.

Elena never broke my heart. She shaped it.

She taught me that love isn't always about getting everything you want, but about discovering what you didn't even know you needed. She showed me that some of the most meaningful connections exist in the spaces between certainty and possibility, in the almost-moments that change you even when they don't resolve into anything you can name.

We didn't have anniversaries or relationship milestones to celebrate. We didn't have a couple photos on social media or plans that extended more than a week or two into the future. What we had was smaller and larger than that—a collection of moments that individually seemed insignificant but together created something that felt essential to who I was becoming.

Like the time she laughed so hard at something I said that she snorted, then immediately covered her nose in embarrassment. "That was so unattractive," she said, mortified.

"That was so real," I replied, and meant it completely.

Or the evening we were walking back from dinner and she stopped suddenly in front of a bookstore window to stare at a novel display. She stood there for so long I thought something was wrong, until she said, "I used to dream about seeing my work displayed like that. Not books—designs. Magazine covers or posters or anything that people might see and think, 'Someone created that. Someone had an idea and made it real.'"

"You still dream about that," I said.

"Sometimes. When I'm brave enough."

"What would it feel like? Seeing your work out there?"

She considered the question seriously, like she always did when I asked her about her hopes rather than her fears. "Like proof that I exist. That I have something worth sharing with the world."

"You already have that."

"How do you know?"

"Because you share it with me."

There were a hundred moments like that. Elena told me about the scar on her knee from falling off her bike when she was seven and how her dad had kissed it better even though she was "too old for that kind of thing." Elena crying at a commercial that featured an elderly couple holding hands, then getting embarrassed about being "ridiculously sentimental." Elena fell asleep during a movie at my place and the way she looked so peaceful that I didn't wake her for an hour.

Each moment was almost. Almost a confession of deeper feeling. Almost a step into something more defined. Almost the beginning of a love story that existed outside the careful boundaries we'd constructed.

But almosts, I learned, could be their own kind of completion.

There was the almost-fight we had in April when Elena got defensive about something I'd said about her work. She'd shown me a design she was particularly proud of, and I'd made what I thought was a constructive suggestion. She'd gone quiet in the way that usually meant she was retreating, and I'd felt the familiar frustration of watching her pull away from connection.

"You don't have to agree with everything I create," she'd said, but her tone suggested she thought I should.

"I wasn't disagreeing. I was engaging. There's a difference."

"Is there? Because it feels like criticism."

"Everything feels like criticism when you're expecting it."

We'd stared at each other across her kitchen table, and I'd seen something flash in her eyes—anger, maybe, or hurt, or both. For a moment, I thought we were about to have our first real fight. Part of me almost wanted it, wanted to push through the careful politeness we sometimes hid behind and find out what we looked like when we stopped being so considerate of each other's feelings.

But then Elena had laughed—not with humor, but with recognition.

"You're right," she'd said. "I am expecting criticism. I expect it from everyone, even you."

"Especially me?"

"Especially you. Because your opinion matters most."

The fight dissolved before it could become anything, but something important had been acknowledged: I mattered to her in a way that was both wonderful and terrifying. My words carried weight. My approval or disapproval could shift her entire sense of herself.

That was its own kind of almost—almost too much responsibility, almost too much influence over someone I cared about deeply.

There was the almost-goodbye when Elena got offered a freelance contract that would have required her to spend three months in Portland. She told me about it over coffee, watching my face carefully as she explained the opportunity and how good it would be for her career.

"Are you going to take it?" I asked, though my heart was already practicing the absence.

"I don't know. It's complicated."

"Because of work here?"

"Because of you."

The admission hung between us like a question neither of us knew how to answer. She was asking me to tell her to stay without actually asking. I was supposed to tell her to go without actually wanting her to.

"You should take it," I said finally. "If it's good for your career, you should take it."

"Should I?"

"Yes. Unless you don't want to."

She studied my face for a long moment. "What do you want, Kota?"

"I want you to make the choice that's right for your life."

"That's not what I asked."

"I want you to stay," I said honestly. "I want you to stay here and keep building whatever this is with me. But I also want you to have the career you dream about and take opportunities that make you grow as an artist. And I don't know how to want both things at the same time."

Elena smiled then—not happily, but with something that looked like relief.

"Thank you," she said.

"For what?"

"For not making it simple. For not pretending your feelings don't matter or that this decision doesn't affect you. For wanting me to stay while still supporting me if I go."

She didn't take the Portland job. Not because I'd asked her not to, but because she realized she didn't want to go. "I'm not running away from opportunities anymore," she told me the next week. "But I'm also not running away from this."

Each almost taught me something. About love, about patience, about the way two people can care for each other without fitting into conventional narratives about how relationships should progress.

Elena was almost who became a beginning. An almost who taught me that not every story needs a dramatic climax to be meaningful. An almost person who showed me that love doesn't always announce itself with fanfare—sometimes it grows quietly in the spaces between what we say and what we mean.

Some hearts get broken.

Mine got shaped.

And that, I realized, was the more valuable transformation.

Poetic Echo

"Though nothing can bring back the hour Of splendour in the grass, of glory in the flower; We will grieve not, rather find Strength in what remains behind."

— William Wordsworth

Chapter 11: Would She Have Loved Me If Timing Was Different?

May

At 2 AM on a Tuesday in mid-May, unable to sleep and caught in one of those late-night spirals where thoughts become their own kind of insomnia, I found myself asking the question that had been living in the corners of my mind for months:

Would Elena have loved me if we'd met at a different time?

Not later—later felt full of possibility, like something we were moving toward rather than away from. But earlier. If we'd met a year before we did, when she was still carrying the weight of her last relationship. Or two years before, when I was still convinced that love was something that happened to other people, something I could observe and write about but never fully experience myself.

If we'd met in college, when we were both still becoming ourselves and might not have recognized what we saw in each other. Or five years from now, when we might both be different people with different needs and fears and ways of moving through the world.

The question felt both pointless and essential. Pointless because we'd met when we'd met, and that timing had led to this—whatever this was—and wondering about alternative timelines was just another way of avoiding the present moment. Essential because it made me think about what Elena and I actually had, what made it work, what made it fragile.

We'd met at exactly the right moment for uncertainty. Elena was just far enough past her last relationship to be open to connection but still close enough to be cautious about it. I was just lonely enough to appreciate what we were building but not so desperate that I'd try to force it into something it wasn't ready to become.

We were both at stages in our lives where we could afford to move slowly, where we had the emotional bandwidth for the careful work of learning to trust each other. If we'd met earlier, would I have had the patience for Elena's careful distances?

Would she have had the space to let me see her fears without feeling like she needed to apologize for them?

I thought about the Elena I'd observed over the months we'd known each other—how she'd grown more comfortable with letting me see her uncertainty, how she'd stopped apologizing for being someone who needed time to trust. How she'd learned to believe that my patience was genuine rather than strategic.

And I thought about how I'd changed too. How loving Elena had taught me that caring for someone doesn't mean trying to fix them or convince them to be different. How I'd learned that the most powerful thing you can offer someone is your presence without conditions, your attention without agenda.

Would either of us have been capable of that kind of love a year earlier? Two years?

The question that kept me awake wasn't really about timing, I realized. It was about worth. Was what Elena and I had meaningful enough to justify the uncertainty, the careful distances, the lack of clear definition? Were we building toward something, or were we just two people who enjoyed each other's company without the courage to admit we wanted more?

I thought about a conversation we'd had the previous week, walking through the farmer's market where we'd bought our plants months earlier. Elena had been telling me about a friend's engagement—how happy she was for her friend, but also how the announcement had made her feel "weird and left behind."

"Do you think about that?" she'd asked. "Marriage, I mean. Not necessarily with me," she'd added quickly, "just in general."

"Sometimes," I'd said honestly. "Do you?"

"I used to think I did. But now I'm not sure if I wanted marriage or if I just wanted proof that someone could love me enough to make that kind of commitment."

"And now?"

"Now I think I want something different. Something that feels more honest and less performative."

"What would that look like?"

She'd stopped to examine a bunch of flowers—sunflowers, bright and open-faced and somehow optimistic. "I think it would look like this," she'd said.

"Like choosing each other repeatedly without needing external validation that the choice is correct. Like building something together because you want to, not because you're supposed to."

"That sounds beautiful."

"It also sounds terrifying. Because it means you have to keep choosing each other even when it's not easy, even when there's no legal or social pressure to stay."

"Is that bad?"

"No," she'd said, buying the sunflowers. "I think it might be the most honest way to love someone."

Lying in bed at 2 AM, remembering that conversation, I realized that Elena and I had been doing exactly what she'd described. We'd been choosing each other repeatedly—not because we were supposed to, not because we'd made any formal commitments, but because what we had felt was worth choosing.

Would she have loved me if the timing was different? Maybe not. Maybe we'd met at exactly the right moment—when we were both ready for the kind of love that doesn't announce itself with certainty, that doesn't demand immediate reciprocation, that grows slowly in the spaces between what we say and what we mean.

Maybe the question wasn't whether Elena would love me under different circumstances, but whether I was brave enough to love her under these circumstances—with all the uncertainty and careful distances and lack of guarantees about where we were heading.

The answer, I realized as I finally started to drift toward sleep, was yes.

Yes, I was brave enough to love someone who was still learning to trust love.

Yes, I was patient enough to build something meaningful in the spaces between friendship and romance.

Yes, I was willing to choose Elena again and again, even when I didn't know if she was choosing me back with the same intentionality.

Because timing isn't just about when you meet someone. It's about being ready for what meeting them will require of you. And for the first time in my life, I was ready for the kind of love that asks you to show up without knowing what you'll receive in return.

I was ready to love Elena exactly as she was, exactly when we'd found each other.

And maybe that readiness was its own kind of perfect timing.

Poetic Echo

"I shut my eyes and all the world drops dead; I lift my eyes and all is born again."

— Sylvia Plath

Chapter 12: Maybe Some Loves Are Meant to Be Written, Not Lived

---

Late May

I started writing about Elena before I knew that's what I was doing.

It began with fragments—observations scribbled in the margins of notebooks, phrases that captured the way afternoon light looked in her hair, attempts to describe the sound of her laugh to myself so I could remember it accurately later. Writing had always been how I processed experiences that felt too large or complex for regular thought, and what I felt for Elena was definitely both.

But somewhere in the midst of trying to capture the essence of our almost-relationship on paper, I started to wonder if maybe that's all it was meant to be. A story. A beautiful, meaningful story that existed primarily in the space between experience and expression, between living and telling.

The thought came to me one evening in late May as I sat in my apartment, working on a scene for my novel that had nothing to do with Elena but somehow kept turning into something that did. Every fictional character I tried to create ended up with her thoughtfulness, her careful way of moving through the world, her ability to find significance in quiet moments.

I set down my pen and looked at the pages I'd filled—ostensibly about characters named Sarah and Michael, but really about the way Elena stirred her coffee counterclockwise, the way she listened to people with her whole body, the way she could make silence feel like conversation.

What if, I thought, this was the point? What if Elena and I weren't building toward some traditional romantic resolution, but were instead creating something more ephemeral and somehow more lasting—a connection that existed primarily in memory and meaning, in the stories we'd tell ourselves about what it felt like to almost love someone perfectly?

The idea should have been depressing. Instead, it felt strangely liberating.

I thought about all the relationships I'd watched friends go through—the dramatic beginnings that faded into routine arguments about dishes and money, the passionate connections that burned bright for six months before dying in mutual exhaustion, the comfortable partnerships that worked on paper but never quite transcended the practical arrangement of shared responsibilities.

What Elena and I had was different. It was all significance and no routine, all meaning and no mundane compromises. We existed in each other's best light, showing up for each other when we were at our most thoughtful and present. We got to love each other without having to negotiate whose turn it was to take out the trash.

Maybe that was enough. Maybe that was everything.

I called my sister that night, needing to test this theory on someone who knew me well enough to tell me if I was rationalizing my way out of something real or into something deeper.

"I think I'm in love with someone I'm never going to actually be with," I told her after the usual pleasantries.

"Okay," Sarah said in the careful tone she used when she was trying not to judge me too quickly. "Tell me about that."

I explained Elena—our months of careful connection, the way we'd built something meaningful in the spaces between friendship and romance, the way she'd become essential to my sense of who I was without ever quite becoming mine in any conventional sense.

"And you think this is... what? A conscious choice on both your parts?"

"I think it might be. I think we might both understand that what we have is too precious to risk by trying to turn it into something more traditional."

"Or," Sarah said gently, "you might both be scared of taking the risk and you're calling that wisdom."

"What's the difference?"

"Intention. Are you choosing to love her this way because it's the most honest expression of what you feel, or because you're afraid of what might happen if you asked for more?"

I thought about that. About the almost-kiss in the park, about the way Elena's face had looked when I told her I loved her, about all the moments when it felt like we were standing at the edge of something deeper but neither of us was quite ready to jump.

"I don't know," I said finally. "Maybe both."

"That's honest, at least."

"Do you think I'm being a coward?"

"I think you're being human. Love is scary, especially the kind that matters. But Kota?"

"Yeah?"

"Don't let fear masquerade as artistic choice. Don't convince yourself that keeping something at a distance makes it more beautiful if what you really want is to get closer."

After we hung up, I sat with Sarah's words for a long time. Was I turning Elena into a muse because that felt safer than asking her to be a girlfriend? Was I romanticizing our uncertainty because I was afraid of what certainty might require of me?

Or was there something genuinely beautiful about a connection that existed primarily in the realm of feeling and meaning rather than practical arrangement and daily compromise?

I thought about Elena's sunflowers from the farmer's market, how she'd put them in a vase by her window where the morning light would hit them first. How she'd told me they made her think of possibility—not specific possibilities, just the general sense that good things could still happen.

Maybe that's what we were to each other. Not a relationship in any traditional sense, but a kind of ongoing possibility. A reminder that connection was real, that understanding was possible, that love could exist without needing to be possessed or defined or guaranteed to last forever.

Maybe some loves are meant to be lived fully in the present tense without worrying about future tense.

Maybe some loves are meant to change you without needing to be forever.

Maybe some loves are meant to be written, not because they're not real, but because writing them is how you honor their particular kind of reality.

That night, I wrote Elena a letter I never intended to send. I told her about all the ways she'd shaped my understanding of what it means to care for another person. I thanked her for teaching me that patience could be its own form of intimacy, that presence could be more powerful than promises.

I told her that loving her had been the most honest thing I'd ever done, even if—or especially because—it was also the most uncertain.

And I told her that if what we had never became anything more than what it was in that moment, it had already been worth it. Already been everything.

I folded the letter and put it in my desk drawer, next to the geode my grandmother had bought me all those years ago. Another beautiful thing that didn't need to be anything other than what it was.

Some loves are meant to be lived.

Others are meant to be written.

And maybe, if you're very lucky, you get to do both.

Poetic Echo

"Love recognizes no barriers. It jumps hurdles, leaps fences, penetrates walls to arrive at its destination full of hope."

— Maya Angelou

Chapter 13: When She Chose to Stay

June 21st - Summer Solstice

It didn't happen suddenly. There wasn't one moment when everything changed, but rather a collection of moments that accumulated like water drops until suddenly there was a stream, then a river, then an ocean of certainty where once there had been only careful hope.

It started with her calling me first more often. Not just returning my calls or responding to my texts, but initiating contact when she had something to share or when she missed me or when she was having the kind of day that felt incomplete without hearing my voice.

"I saw a dog today that looked exactly like it was wearing tiny overalls," she told me one Tuesday morning. "And I immediately wanted to tell you about it, which made me realize I want to tell you about everything. Is that weird?"

"It's not weird," I said. "It's beautiful."

"I was afraid you'd think I was getting clingy."

"I was hoping you were getting attached."

There was a pause, and then her laugh—not the careful, measured laugh she used when she was being polite, but the full, unguarded sound that meant she was genuinely happy.

"Yeah," she said. "I'm definitely getting attached."

Then came the night she showed up at my apartment at 9 PM with takeout containers from the Thai restaurant we'd been meaning to try.

"I was going to eat dinner alone and watch Netflix," she said when I opened the door, looking surprised to see her. "But then I thought about how much better food tastes when you have someone to share it with, and here I am."

We ate pad thai on my couch and watched a documentary about octopuses that Elena had been wanting to see. Halfway through, she shifted to rest her head on my shoulder, and I felt that familiar flutter of contentment that came from her choosing physical closeness without me having to ask for it.

"This is nice," she said during a particularly stunning underwater sequence.

"The documentary?"

"This. Being here with you without having to justify it or analyze it or worry about what it means."

"What does it mean?"

"It means I'm happy," she said simply. "It means I want to be here."

"Where else would you rather be?"

"Nowhere. That's what I'm trying to tell you. There's nowhere else I'd rather be than right here, right now, with you."

The progression was gentle but unmistakable. Elena stopped apologizing for wanting to spend time together. She started making plans that extended further into the future—not dramatic commitments, but casual assumptions that we'd continue to be part of each other's lives. "Next month when we go to that concert," or "This fall we should try hiking that trail you mentioned."

She introduced me to her coworkers at an office happy hour, not with any particular fanfare but with the easy comfort of someone who didn't feel the need to explain or categorize our relationship for other people's benefit.

"This is Kota," she said, her hand briefly touching my arm in a way that felt both natural and significant. "He's..." She paused for just a moment, and I wondered if she was searching for the right label. "He's important to me."

Important. Not boyfriend, not friend, not any of the conventional categories people use to organize their emotional lives. Just important. And somehow that word contained more truth than any official designation could have held.

The shift became undeniable on the summer solstice. Elena had suggested we drive to a nearby lake to watch the sunset on the longest day of the year—something she'd never done but had always wanted to try.

We spread a blanket on the grass near the water's edge and watched the sky turn from blue to pink to gold to deep purple. Other couples and families dotted the shoreline, but we might as well have been alone in the world.

"I used to think that loving someone meant needing them to complete you," Elena said as the first stars began to appear. "Like you were half a person until you found your other half."

"And now?"

"Now I think loving someone means choosing to share your completeness with them. Like you're already whole, but you discover that wholeness feels better when it's witnessed by someone who sees you clearly."

I turned to look at her, and she was already looking at me.

"Is that what this is?" I asked. "Sharing completeness?"

"I think so. I think that's exactly what this is."

She moved closer then, not dramatically but decisively, closing the space between us on the blanket until her shoulder pressed against mine, until I could feel her breathing.

"Kota," she said, and there was something different in her voice. More certain. More present.

"Yeah?"

"I love you."

The words hung in the air between us like a prayer answered, like a question finally receiving its response. Not hurried or desperate or dramatic, but calm and sure and somehow inevitable.

"I love you too," I said. "I have for months."

"I know. And I've been so scared of that—of how much I love you, of how much I want this to work, of how much it would hurt if I lost you."

"You're not going to lose me."

"How do you know?"

"Because I'm choosing you. Every day, I'm choosing you. Not because I have to, not because we've made any promises, but because loving you is the most natural thing I've ever done."

She kissed me then. Finally, after months of almost-kisses and careful distances and the ache of wanting what we weren't sure we were allowed to have.

It was soft and sure and tasted like possibility finally becoming reality. Her hand found mine in the grass, our fingers intertwining as if they'd been practicing for this moment all along.

When we broke apart, Elena was smiling in a way I'd never seen before—open, unguarded, radiant with happiness that didn't seem to contain any shadows of doubt or fear.

"I choose you too," she said. "I choose this. Us. Whatever we want to call it."

"What do we want to call it?"

"Home," she said without hesitation. "I want to call it home."

We stayed by the lake until the moon was bright enough to light our way back to the car, talking about the future not as a series of possibilities but as something we were building together. Elena talked about projects she wanted to work on, places she wanted to travel, the apartment lease she'd been considering renewing.

"Would you want to look at places together?" she asked as we packed up the blanket. "Not necessarily to move in together right away, but to see what's out there. To see what it might feel like to build something more... intentional."

"I'd love that," I said. "I'd love anything that means more time with you."

"Good," she said. "Because I'm planning on sticking around for a while."

"How long is a while?"

"Long enough to find out what happens when two people stop being careful with each other and start being brave."

"That sounds terrifying."

"It sounds perfect."

Driving home that night, Elena's hand in mine, her voice humming along to songs on the radio, I realized that this was what I'd been waiting for without knowing it. Not the dramatic declaration or the passionate beginning, but this: the quiet certainty of someone choosing to stay, choosing to build something lasting and real and honest.

Elena had spent months learning to trust that love didn't have to end badly, that caring for someone didn't have to mean losing yourself, that vulnerability could lead to connection rather than heartbreak.

And I had learned that the most powerful thing you can offer someone isn't the promise of forever, but the commitment to show up fully in each present moment.

She chose to stay. Not because she had to, but because she wanted to.

And that choice changed everything.

Poetic Echo

"The only journey is the one within."

— Rainer Maria Rilke

Chapter 14: A Life Built Softly

Two years later

We didn't fall in love like fireworks exploding across the sky, sudden and bright and impossible to ignore. We grew into love like vines—slowly, steadily, intertwining our lives with such gradual purpose that one day we looked around and realized we'd built something that could weather storms.

Our apartment has morning light that streams through the windows Elena insisted we prioritize when we were house-hunting. She was right, as she usually is about things that matter. The light hits her face as she drinks her first coffee of the day, and I understand why people write poems about ordinary moments that feel miraculous when shared with the right person.

We cook together on weekend mornings—nothing elaborate, just scrambled eggs and toast, maybe pancakes if we're feeling ambitious. Elena is methodical in the kitchen, measuring ingredients with the same careful attention she brings to her design work. I am more improvisational, adding spices by intuition and taste. Somehow our different approaches complement each other, like most things in our life together.

We argue about coffee strength (she likes it strong enough to wake the dead, I prefer mine to taste less like liquid determination) and movie choices (she has inexplicably good taste, I have inexplicably strong opinions about films I haven't seen). We laugh at inside jokes that developed so gradually neither of us can remember their origins.

"Remember when you thought I was just being polite when I said I enjoyed spending time with you?" Elena asked last weekend as we walked through the same farmer's market where we'd bought our first plants.

"Remember when you thought I was too good to be true and kept waiting for me to reveal some terrible character flaw?" I replied.

"Have you revealed any terrible character flaws?"

"You tell me. You're the one who has to live with my habit of leaving coffee cups in random places around the apartment."

"That's not a character flaw. That's just evidence of a creative mind that's too busy thinking about important things to focus on mundane tasks like putting dishes where they belong."

"See? Still too good to be true."

"Still afraid you're going to figure out I'm ordinary and lose interest."

"Still afraid you're going to realize you could do better and upgrade to someone who remembers to put coffee cups in the dishwasher."

"Never going to happen."

"Which part?"

"Any of it."

The silence still exists between us, but now it's comforting—a quiet we sit in without needing to fill it with words or activities or the anxious energy of people who aren't sure they belong together. Sometimes Elena will look up from her laptop where she's working on a design project, catch me watching her, and smile without saying anything. Sometimes I'll reach for her hand while we're watching a movie, and she'll squeeze my fingers in a way that says, "Yes, I'm here, I'm staying, this is real."

She still feels like home, but now it's a home we've built together rather than a feeling I was hoping she might provide. We've painted walls and chosen furniture and argued about whether we need a coffee table (Elena: yes, for functionality; me: no, because I will definitely run into it). We've created rhythms and routines that feel both comfortable and intentional.

Tuesday nights are still for badminton, though we've graduated to a more competitive league and Elena's victory dances have become correspondingly more elaborate. Friday nights are for trying new restaurants or cooking something ambitious at home. Sunday mornings are for coffee in bed and reading different sections of the newspaper and sharing interesting bits of information that may or may not be relevant to each other's lives.

"Did you know," Elena announced last Sunday, "that octopuses have three hearts?"

"I did not know that. Is this information I need for some reason?"

"No, but now you know it, and knowing things together is one of my favorite parts of being with you."

"What are your other favorite parts?"

"The way you listen to me like what I'm saying is the most interesting thing you've heard all day, even when I'm just complaining about a difficult client. The way you make everything feel less scary just by being willing to face it with me. The way you never try to fix my problems unless I ask you to, but you're always willing to sit with me while I figure them out myself."

"Those are pretty specific."

"I've been paying attention."

"What else have you noticed?"

"That you put sugar in your coffee when you're stressed, even though you usually drink it black. That you write better in the morning but you think you write better at night. That you worry about whether you're a good person even though it's obvious to everyone who knows you that you're one of the best people they've ever met."

"You've definitely been paying attention."

"It's easy to pay attention to someone you love."

Love. The word that once felt too big and uncertain to speak aloud now flows naturally in our conversations. Not as a declaration that needs to be reciprocated, but as a simple description of reality. Like saying the sky is blue or coffee tastes better when shared with someone whose company you enjoy.

Elena tells me she loves me when I bring her tea while she's working late on a project. I tell her I love her when she remembers I have an important meeting and texts me encouragement. We say it casually, frequently, not because the feeling has become routine but because we've learned that love expressed regularly becomes a foundation rather than a climax.

"I love you," she said last night as we were brushing our teeth before bed.

"I love you too," I replied, the words as easy as breathing.

"Do you think we'll still say it this easily in twenty years?"

"I think in twenty years we'll probably say it even more easily."

"Promise?"

"Ask me in twenty years."

"I will."

There are no grand speeches in our daily life, no dramatic love letters or elaborate romantic gestures. Just daily proof that we've chosen each other and keep choosing each other. Elena leaves notes in my laptop bag when I'm traveling for work. I surprise her with flowers on random Tuesdays. We take turns planning date nights that range from elaborate (dinner at the new French restaurant downtown) to simple (picnic in the park where we had our first almost-kiss).

Our friends ask us when we're getting engaged, when we're moving to the suburbs, when we're having kids—as if love is a checklist of achievements rather than a daily practice of showing up for each other. We've talked about all of those things, and some of them feel right for our future and some of them don't, but we've learned that the timeline that matters is our own.

"Are you happy?" Elena asked me last month as we were walking home from dinner with another couple who'd spent the entire evening discussing their wedding plans.

"Are you asking because you think I should be unhappy about something?"

"I'm asking because I want to make sure we're building the life you actually want, not just the life you think you're supposed to want."

"I'm happy," I said. "Are you?"

"I'm so happy sometimes I can't believe it's allowed."

"What do you mean?"

"I mean I spent so many years thinking that happiness was something that happened to other people, something I might achieve if I worked hard enough or became good enough or figured out the right combination of choices. But this feels different. This feels like happiness that exists just because we exist together."

"That's the best kind."

"Is it sustainable?"

"We'll find out."

"Together?"

"Together."

This is what love looks like after it stops being a question and becomes a practice. Not the passionate beginning that burns bright and fast, but the steady flame that provides consistent warmth. Not the dramatic story that ends with a wedding and a presumption of forever, but the daily choice to keep building something meaningful with someone who sees you clearly and chooses you anyway.

Elena waters her plants every Sunday morning while I make breakfast. I read her sections of whatever book I'm working on, and she gives me feedback that's both honest and kind. We've learned each other's patterns and preferences so thoroughly that we can navigate shared space without friction, but we still surprise each other regularly enough to stay interesting.

"What do you think we'll be like in ten years?" Elena asked recently as we were lying in bed, her head on my shoulder, both of us too content to be anywhere else.

"Probably pretty similar to how we are now, but with better furniture and more inside jokes."

"That sounds perfect."

"What did you think we'd be like when you first met me?"

"I thought you might be too patient for your own good. I thought I might disappoint you when you realized I was just a regular person with regular problems."

"And what do you think now?"

"Now I think patience is the most radical thing you can offer someone. And I think regular people with regular problems are exactly who deserve to be loved most."

"What about you? What do you think you'll be like in ten years?"

"Braver," she said without hesitation. "More sure of myself. More willing to trust good things when they happen."

"You're already all of those things."

"I'm getting there. You help."

"You help too."

"How?"

"You make me want to be the person you see when you look at me."

"Who do I see?"

"Someone worth loving. Someone worth staying for. Someone worth building a life with."

"You are all of those things."

"So are you."

And that, really, is the most important thing we've built together: the shared understanding that we are both worth the careful work of love. That what we have isn't perfect or dramatic or guaranteed to last forever, but it's real and honest and good enough to invest in daily.

The kind of love that grows in silence—patient, steady, undemanding—turns out to be the kind of love that lasts. Not because it's easy, but because it's sustainable. Not because it doesn't require effort, but because the effort feels worthwhile.

Not because we fell into it, but because we chose it.

And keep choosing it.

Every morning when the light hits Elena's face and she opens her eyes and smiles at me like I'm the best possible way to start her day.

Every evening when we cook together and argue about seasoning and laugh at each other's stories from work.

Every night when we lie in bed talking about everything and nothing until one of us falls asleep mid-sentence and the other pulls the covers up and whispers "I love you" into the darkness.

This is the life we built softly, carefully, together.

And I plan to keep building it with her for as long as she'll let me.

Poetic Echo

"Let yourself be silently drawn by the strange pull of what you really love. It will not lead you astray."

— Rumi

Epilogue: Final Words

If Elena ever reads this—and I hope she does, someday when she's ready to see our story from my perspective—I want her to know that this wasn't written to win her. She's already won. This wasn't written to convince her of anything she doesn't already know in her bones.

This was written to remember her. To remember us. To honor the way she changed me—gently, deeply, without ever demanding that I become someone other than who I was.

Every chapter came from a place I once called hope but now recognize as gratitude. Every silence held her name. Every word was an attempt to capture what it felt like to discover that love doesn't always announce itself with fanfare—sometimes it grows so quietly you don't realize it's taken root until you can't imagine your life without it.

Elena taught me that the most powerful love stories aren't about finding someone who completes you, but about finding someone who witnesses your completeness and chooses to share their own with you.

She taught me that patience isn't passive waiting, but active presence. That kindness isn't a weakness, but the strongest force for changing someone's relationship with themselves and the world.

She taught me that some things are worth the time they take to develop properly—like wine, like friendship, like the kind of trust that allows two people to build something lasting together.

Most importantly, she taught me that love doesn't have to be loud to be real.

The kind of love that grows in silence—the kind that builds slowly in shared glances and comfortable pauses and the gradual recognition that this person makes everything feel more possible—turns out to be the kind of love that changes everything.

It was never waiting to be heard.

It was waiting to be lived.

And now—finally, fully, gratefully—it is.

—Kota

THE END

"The Kind of Love That Grows in Silence" is a work of fiction. Any resemblance to real persons, living or dead, or actual events, is purely coincidental. But the feelings described within these pages? Those are as real as morning light and as true as the choice to love someone exactly as they are.

For everyone who has loved quietly, patiently, without guarantees: your love is revolutionary. Your tenderness is transformative. Your willingness to stay present with uncertainty is the bravest thing you can do.

May you find someone who hears your silence and understands it as the love song it truly is.

THE KIND OF LOVE THAT GROWS IN SILENCE

Somewhere in the quiet spaces
between words and unspoken sighs,
a fragile bond flourished, nurtured
by the gentle touch of time
and the soft murmur of the heart.

www.ingramcontent.com/pod-product-compliance
Ingram Content Group UK Ltd.
Pitfield, Milton Keynes, MK11 3LW, UK
UKHW041352190726
13845UKWH00026B/564